For lost toys everywhere –
may you be safe and found

Bloomsbury Publishing, London, New Delhi, New York and Sydney

First published in the United States of America in 2014 by
Walker Books for Young Readers, an imprint of Bloomsbury Publishing Plc,
1385 Broadway, New York, New York 10018

This edition first published in Great Britain in 2014 by Bloomsbury Publishing Plc,
50 Bedford Square, London, WC1B 3DP

Text and illustrations copyright © Salina Yoon 2013

The moral right of the author/illustrator has been asserted

A CIP catalogue record of this book is available from the British Library

ISBN 978 1 4088 5440 2 (PB)

Printed in China by C&C Offset Printing Co Ltd, Shenzhen, Guangdong

1 3 5 7 9 10 8 6 4 2

www.bloomsbury.com

FOUND

Salina Yoon

BLOOMSBURY

LONDON   NEW DELHI   NEW YORK   SYDNEY

One day, Bear found
something in the forest.

Bear thought it was the most special thing he had ever seen.

He gently carried the toy bunny home.

This lost bunny seems sad, thought Bear.
He wanted to help find its home.

With posters stacked high, Bear set off.

Bear put posters on every tree.

were lost, but not a toy bunny.

He searched high . . .

. . . and low for its owner.

But no one came
for the bunny.

Bear wished the bunny was his to keep.

But the bunny's family must be so worried, thought Bear.

Poor lost bunny!

The next day, Bear and the bunny . . .

swung on a tyre,

played hide-and-seek,

picked juicy blackberries,

and had a picnic.

It was a perfect day,

until . . .

Bear handed the bunny to Moose.

The bunny was finally going home.

As a young calf, Moose had
loved Floppy very much.

Goodbye, Floppy.

Moose was glad to see Floppy,
but special toys are meant to be
passed on to someone special.

"Will you take good care of Floppy for me?" asked Moose.

The bunny wasn't lost any more.

Floppy was home,
safe and
FOUND!